Beep beep! Honk honk! **Vrooom!** *Honk honk!* Wee-oh wee-oh! *Vrooom!* **Wee-oh wee-oh!** BEEP BEEP! **Vrooom!** *Wee-oh wee-oh!* BEEP BEEP! **Honk honk! Beep beep!** *Honk honk!* **Vrooom!** BEEP BEEP! *Honk honk!* **Vrooom!** *Beep beep!* Honk honk! **Vrooom! Honk honk!** *Vrooom!* **Honk honk! Vrooom!** BEEP BEEP! *Wee-oh wee-oh! BEEP BEEP!* **Vrooom!**

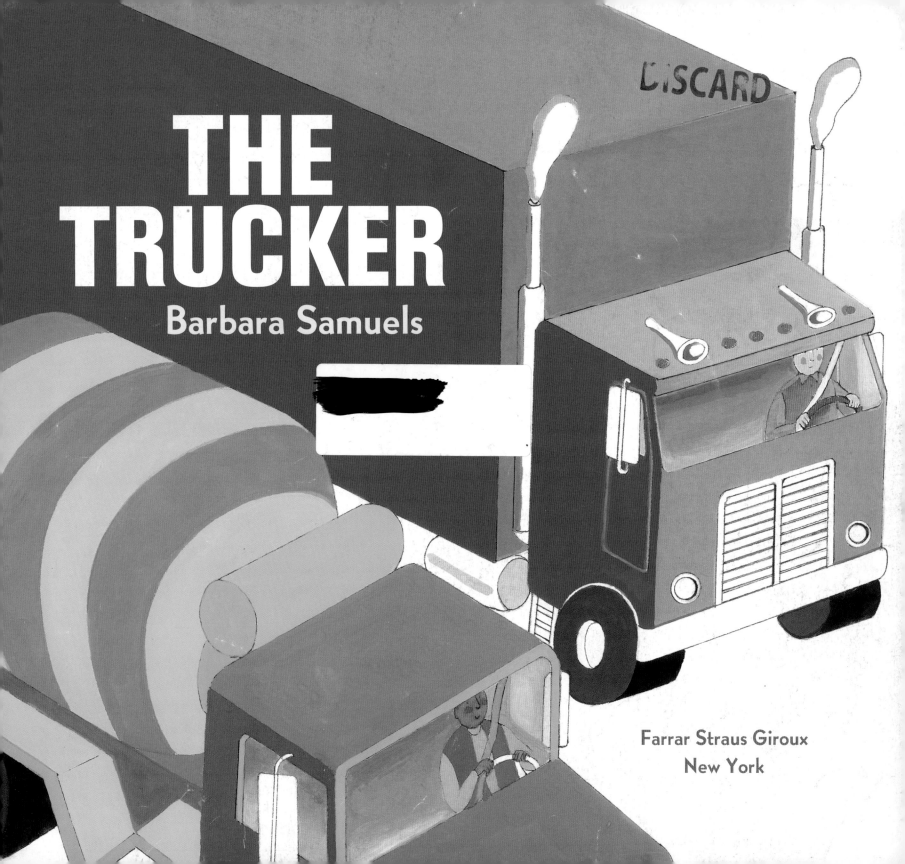

THE TRUCKER

Barbara Samuels

Farrar Straus Giroux

New York

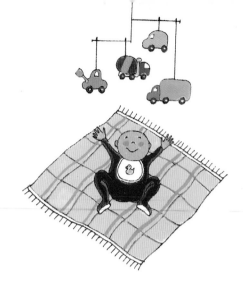

**For my editor, Melanie Kroupa
And for Noah, my favorite trucker**

Distributed in Canada by D&M Publishers, Inc.
Color separations by Embassy Graphics Ltd.
Printed in August 2010 in China by Imago, Shenzen, Guangdong Province
Designed by Jay Colvin
First edition, 2010
3 5 7 9 10 8 6 4 2

www.fsgkidsbooks.com

Library of Congress Cataloging-in-Publication Data
Samuels, Barbara.
    The trucker / Barbara Samuels.— 1st ed.
        p. cm.
    Summary: A boy who loves trucks is disappointed when he receives
a cat named Lola instead of a toy fire truck, but Lola proves to be a
"trucker" after all.
    ISBN: 978-0-374-37804-2
    [1. Trucks—Fiction. 2. Toys—Fiction. 3. Cats—Fiction.] I. Title.

PZ7.S1925Tr 2009
[E]—dc22
                                                    2007029266

From the time he
was very small . . .

VROOOM!

Leo was a trucker.
No doubt about it.

Beep beep!

Time passed. Leo grew bigger. He said
he could name a BILLION trucks.
"I bet you can," said Mama.

One morning Mama noticed that the oatmeal was lumpier than usual.
"Thanks, Mama," said Leo. "I was looking for that pickup truck."

After breakfast, Leo asked
Mama to read his favorite book over and over and over and over and over, until . . .

"It's a beautiful day," said Mama.
"Let's take a walk."

The lady next door was planting tulips.
"So many pretty colors," said Mama.
"Which is your favorite, Leo?"

"I like the green one," Leo said.

While they were walking, they met Leo's friend Sophie.
"Leo," she said, "look how high I can jump!"
"Very, very high!" said Leo.

Something special was
happening on Broadway.

"This one is pretty terrific, don't you think?" asked Mama. "YES!" shouted Leo.

The next day Mama had a surprise
for Leo. He was sure he knew what
it was.

BUT...

"THIS IS NOT A FIRE TRUCK!"

"What shall we call her?" asked Mama.
"She's YOUR cat," said Leo. "YOU name her!"
So Mama did. She called her Lola.

Mama got a nice soft brush.

Lola found a better brush.

Mama bought a catnip toy.
Lola found a better toy.

Mama got a cozy bed.

Lola found a better bed.

No matter where Leo went,
Lola went there, too.

When there was trash to collect,
Lola did it her way.

When a road
needed paving . . .

Lola joined the crew.

And when a building was ready for
the wrecker's ball . . .

KABLAM!

Lola did the job with a swipe of her paw.

WEE-OH! WEE-OH! WEE-OH! WEE-OH! WEE-OH! WEE-OH! WEE-OH! WEE-OH! WEE-OH! WEE-OH! WEE-OH! WEE-OH! WEE-OH!

One day there was a three-alarmer downtown.

Bunny was trapped on the top floor.

Lola was not afraid of heights.

Plunk!

Thunk!

"Not bad," said Leo.
"Let's try that again."

So they did. Afterwards,
Leo made Lola his deputy.

Then it was time to celebrate.

"LOAD 'EM UP!"
said Leo.

"MOVE 'EM OUT!"
And they hauled that heavy load . . .

all the way to Mama's truck stop,
where she cooked it up and served
it fine.

Lola was Leo's cat now.

It was plain to see . . .

She was a trucker.
No doubt about it.

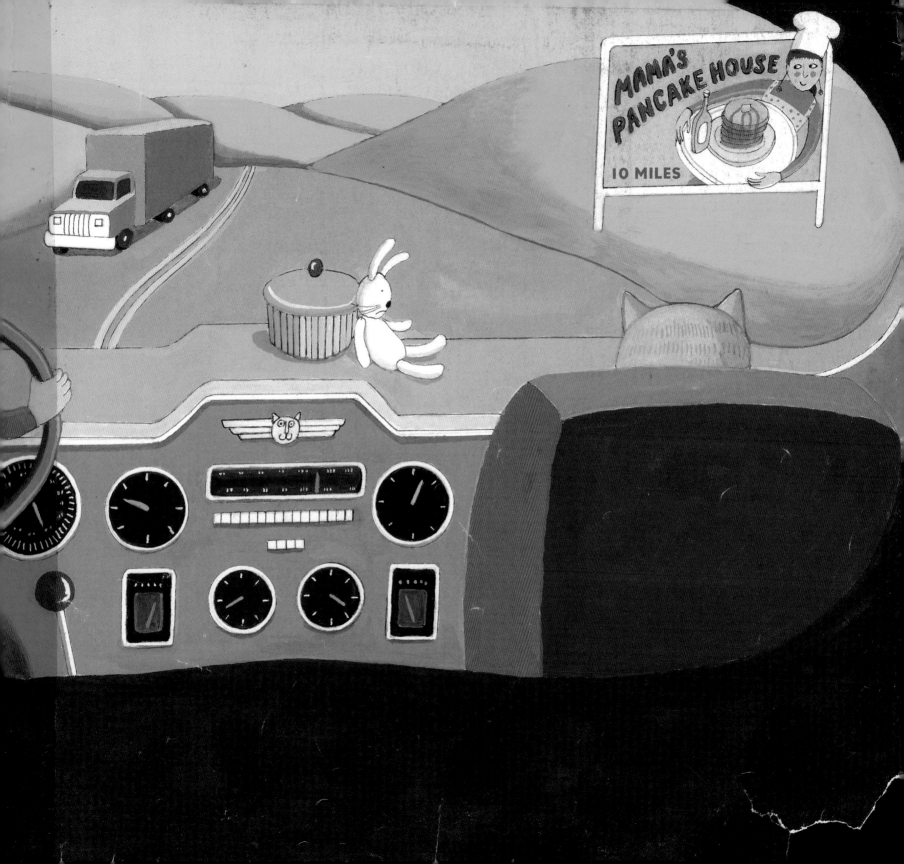

Beep beep! Honk honk! **Vrooom!** *Honk honk!* Wee-oh wee-oh! *Vrooom!* **Wee-oh wee-oh!** BEEP BEEP! **Vrooom!** *Wee-oh wee-oh!* BEEP BEEP! **Honk honk! Beep beep!** *Honk honk!* **Vrooom!** BEEP BEEP! Honk honk! **Vrooom!** *Beep beep!* Honk honk! **Vrooom! Honk honk!** *Vrooom!* **Honk honk! Vrooom!** BEEP BEEP! *Wee-oh wee-oh!* BEEP BEEP! **Vrooom!**